CABINS & CUPIDS

TRASH TO TREASURE COZY MYSTERIES, BOOK 7

DONNA CLANCY

SUMMER PRESCOTT BOOKS PUBLISHING

To my sister, Lynne,
who has always supported me,
and whose love for my children has no limits.

ONE

"Four days of skiing, sitting in front of a warm fire with a big mug of hot chocolate and no thoughts of work," Gabby said, loading her suitcase in the back of Cliff's mother's SUV. "It doesn't get any better than that."

"Set your skis up against the car and I'll strap them on the roof rack," Cliff said.

"I have Rory's skis here, too," Gabby replied. "I'll be right back."

"This is going to be awesome," Sage said. "I've never been skiing before."

"I guess this is the sheriff's way of thanking us for inviting him to be with us over the holidays. I didn't know he had a cabin up in the mountains much less one that sleeps twelve people," Cliff stated, putting Rory's suitcase in the back of the car.

"He said he rents it out most of the time, and only uses it three or four times a year. With the new snowfall coming, he figured we may like to go skiing. The Perry Slopes are only two miles from the cabin, and they have a bunny slope for us newbies," Sage said.

Gabby returned with Rory's skis, and they were added to the ones already on the roof of the car. They piled in and were going to stop at Rory's construction company to pick him up for the trip.

"So, do we know who's going to be there for the long weekend?" Gabby asked.

"The four of us, the sheriff, my mom, and Barry Steiner," Sage replied.

"Who's Barry Steiner?" Cliff asked.

"He's the sheriff's next-door neighbor. He has taken Barry skiing with him before, so he invited him to go along for the weekend," Sage replied. "I believe he's a junior at Cupston High School."

"I didn't know your mom liked to ski," Gabby said.

"She loves it. She's been skiing since she was a young girl. I never got into it because she always went with her friends, and I didn't want to be the only kid there. Although, it has been a while since she went because her friends who she skied with have since moved away."

"It seems your mom and the sheriff have struck up quite the friendship," Gabby said.

"They've always been friends, since elementary school. My mom knows what it's like to be lonely. People in this town turned on her after her divorce and she spent many nights in her room crying. She never knew I heard her, but I would lay in my bed listening to her. She doesn't want the sheriff to feel isolated or lonely like she did."

"Your mom is good people," Cliff said. "There's Rory. He's actually ready on time."

"This weekend is all he has talked about. The Sharp house that he finally managed to get the permits for has been one problem after another. I think he's happy to be getting away for a few days."

"I'm so ready to hit the slopes," Rory said, climbing into the car.

"The cabin is about an hour away on the north side of Perry Mountain. Everyone else is going to meet us there," Sage replied. "My mom and Barry are riding up with the sheriff."

"Before we get too far out of town, does anyone want coffee?" Cliff asked.

Everyone said they wanted coffee so Cliff pulled into the Cupston Café and parked. The guys stayed in the car while the women went in to get the order. Gabby left for the ladies room one more time before the trip while Sage stood in line waiting to place their order.

Sage looked around not recognizing many of the faces in the café. It was ski season and Cupston was a short distance from one of the local slopes so there were many outsiders in the area. She turned to see how many more people were in front of her in line and was bumped from behind. Turning, a woman she had never seen before was right in her face.

"Tell your mom to be careful this weekend," she whispered, before rushing off out the door.

Sage chased her but lost her in the parking lot. She ran to the SUV and asked the guys if they had seen the woman as she exited the café, but they hadn't. Gabby was standing at the door looking befuddled.

"Did you get our stuff?" she asked Sage as she reentered the café.

"No, I'm sorry. I had to get out of line."

She told Gabby what had happened and that she tried to chase the woman to find out what she meant but lost her once she got out the door. They got back in line again.

"That's strange," Gabby replied. "Was it meant to be a threat or a warning?"

"I don't know."

"And you're sure you don't know who the woman was."

"I've never seen her before and, unfortunately, this place has no security cameras. We're next."

They collected their order and returned to the car. Sage relayed what happened to the guys while they ate their warm apple fritters and drank their coffee. They all agreed not to tell Sarah what happened, but they would tell the sheriff. All four promised to keep a close watch on her over the long weekend.

Sage tried to be cheerful on the way to the cabin and not bring the others down, but she was worried about her mom. Was it a warning or a threat, and if a threat, from who? Cliff squeezed her hand, sensing she was upset. She smiled and he smiled back.

"Don't you worry," he said. "We'll protect Sarah no matter what."

"I know you will. I'm trying to figure out who knew where we were going this weekend."

"You don't know who your mom told," Cliff replied.

"But, why, all of a sudden, would someone want to hurt her?" Sage asked. "And for what reason?"

"I don't have an answer for you. There's a lot of strange people in the world and you never know when you will cross paths with them," Cliff stated. "It's scary."

"Try not to worry about it," Gabby piped up from the back seat. "She might have been a whack job and doesn't even know your mom. When we get to the cabin, talk to the sheriff, and see what he thinks."

"Speaking of," Sage said, looking at her phone. "The sheriff says he invited Deputy Bell and his fiancé to join us. He hopes we don't mind."

Sage messaged him back and said they were happy to spend some time with him outside a professional capacity. She told the sheriff they were about twenty minutes away.

"Another cop around to protect your mom. That's a good thing," Cliff said. "Now relax and try to enjoy yourself this weekend."

Cliff drove up the winding road on the side of Perry Mountain. It was slippery in spots from the previous night's snow and several times he had to slow to a crawl to stay on the road. They missed the dirt road leading to the cabin and had to ask directions. Ten minutes later they arrived at the cabin and were greeted by Sarah and the sheriff as they came out the front door to get wood for the fireplace.

"You made it," Sarah said, giving her daughter a hug. "Wait until you see this place. It's gorgeous."

"You'd better bring in all your stuff as they are calling for more snow later tonight and early in the morning. Later in the day the sun is supposed to be out, and it will be a perfect day for skiing with fresh snow," the sheriff said. "You can put your skis and boots in the mudroom off the kitchen."

The car was emptied, requiring two trips to get everything inside. Barry was inside, sitting in an over-stuffed chair, playing a video game on the large screen TV that hung over the fireplace.

"This is Barry Steiner," Sarah announced, making the necessary introductions.

"I'm going out and get more firewood. Any helpers?" the sheriff asked.

"I'll go," Sage said. "So will Cliff."

He led them to the firewood that was stacked in neat piles behind the house.

"Sheriff White, before we bring in the wood, I have something I need to talk to you about," Sage said.

"Please, as I have said before, call me Gerald. We are all adults now."

She told him what happened at the café and that she didn't know if it was a threat or a warning. He listened to everything she had to say before he spoke.

"And you didn't know who this woman was?"

"No, I have never seen her before."

"This is what we are going to do. Don't breathe a word of this to your mother. I don't want her looking over her shoulder all weekend out of fear. And don't say anything in front of Barry. I will tell Bell what's going on when he gets here and the both of us will keep our eyes open for anything suspicious."

"And we'll do the same," Cliff said.

They loaded up their arms with wood and went back into the house. After they piled it in the holders near the fireplace, Gerald decided one more trip was needed to be fully stocked for the incoming storm. This time Sage stayed inside, and Rory went out for the second trip.

"How's it feel to be on vacation?" Sage asked her mom. "Even if it's only for a few days."

"I'm loving it. It was so nice of Gerald to ask me to come with him. I haven't been skiing in years and really miss it. Sage, would you make sure the teakettle on top of the wood stove has enough water in it," Sarah requested.

"Sure, not a problem."

"Where did Barry go?" Sage asked, returning with a full kettle of water. "He seems like a good kid."

"He went out to help with the wood. Gerald took me aside and said as long as he's known Carol, his mother, she's always been overbearing. He takes Barry up here as often as he can to give him a break from her."

"It makes you feel sorry for him, doesn't it?" Sage whispered.

"Gerald said the rumor has always been her husband left her for that very reason."

"What are you two whispering about?" Gerald asked, walking to the woodstove area with an armload of wood, dumping it in the holder and turning to go outside for another load.

"Nothing in particular," Sage answered quickly, seeing Barry following right behind him. "So, Barry, do you like to ski?"

"I love skiing. The only time I get to go is when Sheriff White invites me to come to the cabin. Plus, I get to get away from my mom for a while which is a total bonus," Barry replied, watching the sheriff walk out the door. "He's an awesome dude."

"Yes, he is," Sarah agreed. "Sage, let me show you and Gabby where you are sleeping."

Sarah led them to a bedroom which had three sets of bunkbeds. Two bureaus, one on either end of the room, were available if anyone didn't want to live out of their suitcase while they were there.

"I have that bottom bunk," Sarah said, pointing to the one closest to the door. "You girls can pick from what's left over. And when Bell and his fiancé get here, she can pick from the remaining ones. I think her name is Shelly."

"It is Shelly. She's really nice. I went to school with her," Gabby replied. "I choose this bunk, if that's okay with you Sage."

"That's fine. I'll take the one above you, so Shelly has a choice between a top or bottom bunk," Sage said.

"Good! You girls get settled in and I'll meet you out in front of the fire for a glass of wine," Sarah said, closing the bedroom door behind her.

Sage was glad they had a little privacy. She told Gabby what the sheriff said about the lady in the café and what her mother said about Carol. They agreed to watch over Sarah while out on the slopes. They set their suitcases at the foot of their beds and put on their warm, fuzzy slippers.

"Now let's go have a glass of wine with my mom."

Bell and his fiancé arrived an hour later right before it started to snow. Gerald had done food shopping, along with beer, and soda for the weekend. Everyone pitched in and gave him some money for their share of the groceries and drinks. As the storm raged, Gerald cooked hamburgers and hotdogs on the grill outside which was tucked under the porch roof.

Condiments, chips, salads, and rolls were set buffet style on the counter in the kitchen. Everyone was going to use paper plates which would make cleaning up easier. Gerald returned with the cooked meats. The younger people sat on the floor in front of the fireplace while the older people sat on the couch.

"Sheriff White, is it okay if I play video games while I eat?" Barry asked.

"Sure, you're on vacation, too," he answered. "Just don't tell your mother I let you play them."

"I won't. I promise," he said, heading back to the kitchen for seconds.

"She won't even let him play video games?" Cliff whispered. "What a grinch."

Barry stopped and turned to look at Cliff.

"I'm sorry, we shouldn't have been talking about your mother like we were," Sage said.

"I'm sorry I called her a grinch. It's just everybody your age plays video games," Cliff said.

"It's okay. You're not the first ones and won't be the last ones. I was so mad when she tried to invite herself to come along this weekend. This is my place to go. Sheriff White has always been so nice to me and treats me like an adult when we're here. She'd have ruined everything by coming."

"You can hang around with us and go skiing when we go, unless you want to go with the sheriff and my mother. Does your mother like to ski?" Sage asked.

"No, which makes it hard to understand why she even wanted to come," Barry replied.

"I'm sorry," Sage replied. "The offer stands if you want to join us on the slopes. I'll be on the bunny trail, but you can ski with the others."

"Thanks, I appreciate it," he said, strolling off to the kitchen.

"Poor kid," Gerald said. "That's why I bring him up here. With no dad around, a guy needs his space."

"She doesn't even ski. It makes no sense she wanted to come up here," Sage replied.

"We'll have to do our best to keep him out on the slopes so he enjoys himself," Cliff said. "I'm heading to the kitchen for seconds. Do you need anything?"

"No thanks, one plateful is enough for me."

"The storm is ramping up outside," Rory said, putting more wood on the fire. "There ought to be a good foot of fresh snow on the slopes in the morning. The sheriff picked a great weekend to go skiing."

"Please, you're all old enough to call me Gerald. I am the sheriff in a professional capacity but up here I'm Gerald," he said, entering the room from the kitchen. "And that includes all of you."

"I don't know if I can do that, sir," Andy stated. "You're still my boss."

"Up here, I'm just another friend, and you can call me Gerald."

"Yes, sir, I mean Gerald," Andy said, smiling.

"I'll be on my bunk reading. Call me when everyone is done eating so I can help clean up the kitchen," Shelly said, pouring herself more wine and heading to the bunkroom where it was quiet for reading.

Half an hour later, everyone had finished eating. Sage and Gabby cleaned the kitchen without bothering Shelly while she read. Everyone else participated in some board games. The fire roared and marshmallows were toasted. Ski stories were exchanged along with much laughter and teasing. It was decided Sage would definitely have to start her day on the bunny slopes.

Outside, the wind blew, and the snow piled up. The doors to the bunk rooms were kept open so the heat could circulate from the fireplace. The guys went outside and stood on the porch near the grill while the sheriff smoked his annual vacation cigar.

The women were sitting in front of the fire, chatting, and enjoying mugs of steaming hot chocolate with mini marshmallows. Shelly came out of the bedroom and stopped at the door. Instead of joining the women, she glanced their way and went outside to find her fiancé. She came back in several minutes later and said good night. She apologized for going to bed so early but had been up since three that morning and was tired.

"Good night," Barry said, coming in from outside. "It looks like we will need to be up early to shovel our way out of here so we can go skiing."

"See you in the morning," Sarah replied, watching him walk into the men's bunk room. "I feel so bad for him sometimes."

"Why do you say that?" Gabby asked.

"His mother is a strange duck," Sarah answered in a hushed tone.

"Have you dealt with Carol Steiner much?" Sage asked.

"I see her every time I go to Gerald's house."

"What do you mean?" Gabby asked.

"Whenever I visit Gerald, whether it's personal or on a town matter, she comes out of the house and finds a reason to visit him while I'm there," Sarah replied.

"It sounds like she doesn't want you alone with the sheriff," Gabby commented. "Maybe she's jealous of your friendship."

"But that's all it is, a friendship," Sarah said in protest. "Why would she think it's anything else?"

"Maybe living next door she's had her eye on Gerald since her husband left her. And when his wife died she saw her chance to move in," Gabby said.

"That's crazy. Gerald can't stand to be around her because she's so pushy; he's told me so himself," Sarah replied.

"Ahh, Mom," Sage said, tilting her head toward the kitchen.

Sarah turned around to see Barry standing there, holding a soda bottle, listening to every word they were saying. He frowned and hurried back to the bunk room.

"Maybe I better go talk to him," Sarah said, standing up.

"Do you think that's a good thing to do?" Sage asked her mom. "Maybe Gerald should talk to him and tell him there is nothing between them but being neighbors all these years."

"I'd better go speak to Gerald in private," Sarah said, grabbing her coat.

"Barry was right," Gabby said. "She's not even here and she's going to screw up the weekend for everyone."

The guys came in from outside so Sarah could speak with Gerald privately. They crowded in front of the fire to warm up. Sage offered them hot chocolate, but they all decided on a beer instead. Sarah joined them a short time later. Gerald knocked on the door and went in to talk to Barry. When he came out, he motioned for Sarah to join him in the kitchen.

"I hope everything's okay," Sage whispered to Gabby.

TWO

"What's going on?" Cliff asked.

"I'm not sure," Sage replied.

"I'm sure it has something to do with my mother," Barry said, coming out of the bunk room after his conversation with Gerald.

"I'll just be glad when tomorrow gets here and we can get out on the slopes and away from the inside drama," Gabby stated.

"You and me both," Barry mumbled, heading for the kitchen.

Sarah came out of the kitchen and sat down next to her daughter. They waited for her to speak but she didn't say anything.

"What's going on, Mom?"

"Nothing. We have decided to concentrate on skiing for the rest of the weekend," Sarah replied. "No more drama, just relaxing."

"I just said that very thing, about the drama, I mean," Gabby said.

"Gerald says Barry is a phenomenal skier, and you can tell he is in another world when he is out on the slopes. He wants Barry to have a good time while he is here."

Barry returned to his room with a bag of chips and another soda. Gerald grabbed his beer and joined Sarah on the couch. They spoke quietly between themselves, and Sarah smiled.

"Now, I'm going to say goodnight so I can be up early to shovel us out so we can get to the slopes. I'll see everyone in the morning. Doors are all secured and there is plenty of firewood inside for those who want to stay up a while and enjoy the fire," he said, finishing his beer.

"Goodnight, Gerald," Sarah said.

"We can all get up and help," Cliff offered. "I'll be in as soon as I finish my beer."

"I guess we women can man the kitchen and cook everyone a good breakfast before we go skiing," Sarah replied. "Scrambled eggs, bacon, pancakes, and lots of steaming hot coffee."

"Can we eat before we shovel?" Rory asked.

"Coffee, yes, food no," Sarah replied, laughing.

"You're not even married yet and she's bossing you around," Cliff said, teasing his best friend.

"I heard that," Gabby replied, walking to the bunk room.

The guys were laughing as the women marched to the other room to go to bed.

"Double check to make sure everything is locked up before you go to bed," Sage said to Cliff, before propping the door open for heat circulation.

"Who in their right mind is going to be out in this storm?" Cliff asked.

"You never know," Sage started to say when a huge bang sounded at the back of the cabin. "What was that?"

Gerald came flying out of the other room as well as the other women.

"Is everyone okay?" he asked.

"I think so. It sounded like it came from the back of the cabin," Cliff replied.

They pushed their way through the back door. The plastic roof protecting the grill and back door area had collapsed under the weight of the falling snow. It took three of the men to hold up the plastic and push on it from below to flip the snow off and clear the door. Gerald brushed the snow off the grill and threw the cover over it, tying it down to keep it in place in the high winds.

Cliff and Rory dragged the ridged plastic sheet into the mud room so it didn't blow away and they could re-attach the roofing when the storm blew over. There was nothing else that could be done until morning, so they all went to bed.

Sage laid in bed listening to the storm raging around the cabin. Inside, the snoring coming from Shelly's bed was the only sound she could hear above the wind. The windows rattled as the snow was slammed up against them and sometimes it sounded like they were going to pop right out of the wall.

The heat continued to circulate as they slept. The fire in the fireplace had died to glowing embers but the woodstove was full to the brim to keep it burning through the night. The teakettle on top of the wood stove released a steady stream of steam which kept moisture in the air.

Tomorrow they would all hit the advanced slopes, except for Sage, who would be on the bunny slopes. Looking back, she wished she had learned to ski when she was younger and her mom had offered to take her when she went with her friends.

She didn't like the fact she wouldn't be near her mother to watch out for her while she whipped down the slopes. The only saving grace in her mind was Gerald, Cliff, and Rory would be near her should something happen.

Why didn't I react faster and catch that woman before she slipped away without finding out what she meant? Did she issue a threat or a warning? This is so darn frustrating.

An extra powerful gust of wind made the window near to Sage's bunk rattle fiercely. She turned to watch to make sure it was going to stay put in the wall when she saw something she wished she hadn't.

"Cliff!" she screamed, jumping out of bed.

The men all came running and Sage's scream woke up everyone around her. The face in the window disappeared.

"What's the matter?" Cliff asked, fighting to get his arm in the sleeve of his robe.

"That window, right there. Someone was looking in the cabin and now they're gone."

"Seriously? In this storm?" Shelly mumbled, half asleep.

"Yes, seriously," Sage replied.

"Are you sure you weren't dreaming?" her mother asked.

"I was wide awake, and there was a face looking in the window. It had a black ski mask on with a fur hat that had the ear flaps pulled down over the ears. Blue tinted goggles covered the eye area. It was definitely there," Sage insisted.

"Why would anyone in their right mind be out in this storm?" Gabby asked.

"If they were lost and needed shelter, why didn't they come to the door and ask to be let in?" Barry added. "It doesn't make any sense."

"In all my years of coming to the cabin I have never had anything like this happen," Gerald stated. "I'm going to get dressed and look around outside. If someone was there, they should have left tracks in the snow. Anyone game to go out in the storm with me?"

"I'll go," Andy replied.

"Me, too," Cliff said.

The three men disappeared into the bunk room to get dressed. Minutes later they were pushing their way through the snow to get out the back door. Sage tried to watch through the window, but the clinging snow made it difficult to see more than a few feet away from the cabin. In the darkness, she saw the men returning to the back door and was there to meet them.

"Well? Did you see anything?" she asked as they took off their wet, snow-caked clothes.

"Even with the wind blowing as hard as it is, there were definite tracks to the window and then away again. Sage was right. Someone was at the window," Gerald replied.

"We were going to try to follow them but without a strong lantern it would have been impossible once we got out into the woods surrounding the cabin," Andy stated.

"For the life of me I can't figure out what kind of fool would be out in this weather," Sarah said. "I hope they have some kind of shelter nearby and don't freeze out there overnight."

"Whoever it was is gone now. I'm going to check the doors again to make sure everything is secure," Gerald said. "Why don't you all go back to bed and try to get in a few hours of sleep?"

"I'm not tired," Sage replied. "Do you mind if I start up the fire in the fireplace? The embers are still orange, and it should be easy to get it going again."

"Sure, but if you go to bed make sure the screen is in front of it," Gerald answered.

"I won't be going to bed for a while," Sage replied. "But I will put the screen in front of it as soon as I have the fire going."

"Do you want me to stay up with you?" Cliff asked.

"No, go get some sleep. You'll need all your energy for skiing tomorrow. And before you ask, Mom, you go back to bed, too," Sage replied. "I'm going to pour some boiling water out of the kettle on the wood-stove and make myself a nice cup of tea and sit in front of the fire."

"Make sure you replace the water you use," Gerald said. "I wouldn't want the kettle to boil dry."

"I will."

"On second thought, Sage, I'll start the fire if you check the status of the doors."

"Will do."

"And Sarah, we need to talk. You, me and your daughter. Grab a glass of wine or tea and we'll all meet in front of the fireplace in a few minutes."

Sage knew what was going to be said. After someone had been outside the cabin, she knew that this was serious and the warning she had been given could not be taken lightly anymore. Her mom had to be told of the situation so she could be on her guard, too.

"I want to have this conversation at a quiet level because I don't want Barry to know what is going on," Gerald started. "It might scare him."

"Exactly what is going on?" Sarah asked.

Between Gerald and Sage, Sarah was told about everything concerning her and the warning or threat. She sat in silence, listening intently, her face showing no expression at all.

"I need more wine," Sarah said, getting up from the couch.

Sage and Gerald looked at each other. Did Sarah not understand the gravity of the situation? He got up and added more wood to the fire while waiting for Sarah to return from the kitchen. She returned and sat back down next to Gerald on the couch.

"I've done some thinking while I was in the kitchen. I have no idea who it is that would want to hurt me or why. Gerald, I want you to take me to a hotel first thing in the morning when the roads are plowed. I don't want to endanger anyone here or ruin the weekend for everyone else. It's not up for debate."

"That's not happening," Sage blurted out. "We can't keep an eye on you at a hotel miles away like we can here. You're staying put."

"I have to agree with Sage," Gerald said, putting his hand on top of Sarah's. "Everyone can protect you here in the cabin, and I will never be that far away from you while we are out on the slopes. Once day breaks, I am going to see if I can follow the tracks leading away from the window. The wind might fill them in overnight, but we'll see."

"Do the others know?" Sarah asked.

"Everyone but Barry," Gerald replied.

"Think back. Who knew you were coming up to the cabin this weekend?" Sage asked her mom. "Did anyone seem overly interested in your skiing trip?"

"The only people who knew I was leaving for a few days was Flora and her fiancé. She had to know because she was going to watch the store for me."

"Could any customers have overheard you talking about it?" Gerald asked.

"They could have, I don't know, but it still comes down to the point I don't know anyone who is mad at me or would want to hurt me," Sarah said.

"Sage, you're positive you've never seen the woman who spoke to you in the café?" Gerald asked

"Never."

"Well, I did come up to get some skiing in, and if everyone is going to be on the lookout for me, I feel safe. I can't let a when and if take away my good time. I'm not one to hide or backdown, so I guess running away to a hotel is kind of dumb. I don't get away from the store very often and who knows when I'll get to go skiing again."

"Does that mean you'll stay?" Gerald asked, smiling.

"I'll stay," Sarah said, returning his smile and finishing her last little bit of wine. "Now can we go to bed? It's two a.m."

"I'm going to sit here in front of the fire and finish my tea," Sage replied. "I'll see you in the morning."

"Don't stay up too long," Sarah said. "Good night, Gerald."

"Good night. Don't you worry. We won't let anything happen to you," he promised.

Sage was left alone in the living room. The fire crackled and it felt warm on her feet. She finished her tea and set the mug on the floor next to the chair. She closed her eyes, trying to think of any little detail she could remember about the woman at the café. Between the late time and the warmth of the fire, she dozed off.

She was awakened at seven when the guys came out of their bunk room teasing each other as to who would be the first to wipe-out when skiing. They didn't know she was sleeping there and apologized for waking her up. Sage brushed it off and got up to start the coffee brewing. Gerald stoked the fire in the fireplace, filled the woodstove with a fresh load of wood and the cabin was warm in no time.

The first shift consisting of Gerald and Andy bundled up and went outside to start shoveling. There were only two shovels, so the guys rotated and shoveled in half-hour shifts. When Cliff and Barry took over for the second shift, Sage watched Gerald and his deputy head off into the woods to try to follow the trail in the snow from the previous night.

The front of the cabin and the driveway were clear by the time the plow came along and cleared the dirt road leading out to the main road. It left a wall of snow at the foot of the driveway that had to be shoveled out for a second time. The rest of the women had come out dressed and ready to cook breakfast for the guys.

Sage stayed near the coffee maker, making sure there was plenty of coffee on hand all the while keeping an eye on the window. Gabby and Sarah had gone out the back door of the cabin to work on clearing off the grill and its surrounding area before the guys put the roof back up.

The guys decided to eat before they attached the roof on the back of the cabin. They all took full plates and full cups of hot, steaming coffee and sat on the hearth of the fireplace. Scrambled eggs, bacon, ham and home fries were on the menu. A tower of buttered toast sat next to the toaster on the kitchen counter for everyone to help themselves to.

"I forgot the orange juice in the back of the car," Gerald said. "Sage, will you help me bring in the groceries that are left in the car?"

"Sure," she replied, pulling on her boots.

The two headed to the car, Sage figuring he wanted to tell her in private what they found in the woods. Gerald handed her a bag of groceries, grabbed a second bag himself, and closed the rear hatch of his vehicle.

"We followed the trail the person at the window made last night. Unfortunately, we lost it a few hundred feet into the woods. I don't know of any other cabins anywhere close to this one where someone could have gone for shelter. I'm really worried about what kind of person we are dealing with here."

"He's either some kind of nutcase taking a chance being out in the storm or he's a survivalist. And if that's the case, I'm really worried about my mom's safety."

"Your mom will be with one of us at all times."

"We better head back in before Mom comes out looking for us and wants to know what's going on," Sage said. "I think I'm going to pass on the bunny slopes today and stick around the cabin. I don't want all our belongings to be left here unguarded or the cabin left deserted for someone to get into while no one is here."

"You're going to pass on skiing?"

"I can ski next time. The bunny slopes are not quite the same thing as the skiing like you guys do. As long as I know you are with my mom, I can stay here and guard the fort, as they say."

"There will be a next time, I promise, and there'll be no drama to ruin it for everyone."

"I can't wait for that weekend," Sage said, smiling.

While finishing breakfast, they heard the plows drive by outside a second time, widening the road for the group to get out to go skiing. The guys went back outside to clear the end of the driveway again, but this time it wasn't as bad as the last time and the plow's residual was cleared away in no time at all.

Sage pulled her mom aside to talk to her in private. She told her mother she was staying at the cabin and would not join them skiing. Not wanting Barry to be suspicious, Sage would feign a stomachache and claim she wanted to sit by the fire and read or lay down when she felt like it.

"I'm sorry you're not feeling well. The snow is perfect for skiing," Barry said to Sage. "Even for newbies on the bunny slopes."

"Thank you. Maybe next time or even tomorrow," Sage said, smiling at being called a newbie.

"Everyone ready to go? The skis are on the roof rack and the rest of the gear is in the SUV. I think we can all fit in one vehicle seeing as Sage isn't going with us," Gerald said. "If you don't want to be so squished, we can take two vehicles."

It was decided they would take two vehicles as the number of people and the thick ski suits they were wearing would make for an uncomfortable ride. The boots and other equipment were left in the back of Gerald's SUV.

"You take it easy today," Sarah told her daughter, winking at the same time.

"I will, Mom. Have an awesome time skiing," Sage replied. "I'll be in front of the nice warm fire, drinking my tea and reading my new book I brought with me."

"Are you sure you don't want me to stay with you?" Cliff asked his girlfriend.

"No, you go and enjoy yourself. I'll be fine," Sage answered, knowing her mom would tell him the real reason she stayed at the cabin when they were alone and not anywhere near Barry for him to hear.

Sage watched them pile into the cars. She laughed as she thought they each looked like the marshmallow man they had seen in a movie they watched at Halloween. The car drove off and she closed and locked the door.

I hope they have a good time.

The day passed quickly as Sage buried herself in her reading. A little after three, Sage heard a vehicle pull into the driveway. She walked to the door and saw only her mom and Gerald in the SUV. She grabbed a sweater that was hanging next to the door and ran out to see where everyone else was.

"Don't panic, your mom is fine," Gerald said, getting out of the driver's side door.

"What do mean my mom is fine?" Sage replied, her voice rising in fear.

"There was an accident on the slopes. A skier dressed all in black shot out of the trees and cut Sarah off. She swerved to avoid hitting him and ended up in the trees on the other side of the slope," Gerald replied, opening the door for Sarah.

"I'm fine," her mother said. "I was lucky and only ended up with a fractured ankle. It could have been a lot worse. They x-rayed it at the hospital and put a cast on it. Unfortunately, my skiing for this trip is done and over with."

"What do you mean someone cut you off? Deliberately?"

"I was a short distance behind your mom and from what I witnessed; it was done on purpose. He shot out of the woods on a direct course for Sarah. If your mom wasn't such a great skier, things *could* have been a lot worse. I watched her dodge trees and large boulders like an Olympic skier."

"I finally found a small clearing and threw myself down in a small snowbank to stop myself from going any further. My skis went one way, and I went another. That's how my ankle got fractured," Sarah said, struggling to get out of the car.

"Let me help you," Sage offered, stepping forward.

"You take her crutches. I have her," Gerald said, passing off the crutches to Sage and picking Sarah up in his arms. "Let's get you in on the couch."

They situated Sarah in front to the fireplace, placing several pillows under her cast.

"Do you want a glass of wine?" Sage asked.

"I'd love a glass, but I can't. They gave me some painkillers and I don't think they would mix very well. I could use a nice cup of tea."

"Coming right up," Sage said. "Where are the others?"

"I left them at the slopes. They were going to walk around the parking lots and see if they could find the person dressed in black who did this to Sarah. I'm supposed to go back and join them as soon as I'm done here."

"I'll watch my mom so you can go back to the lodge," Sage replied.

"They'll be fine. I'm supposed to meet them in the ski lodge near the main fireplace. They were all meeting back there after they looked around."

"It's too bad the cell phone reception is so bad up here. We could call them to see what is happening, if anything at all," Sage said.

"The cells work fine at the lodge. There is a cell tower on top of the mountain. My cabin is too far away from the tower to get any reception. The phones start working again halfway up to the ski lodge."

"I'll be fine. We'll start supper while you are gone," Sarah said.

"I'll start supper while you are gone. My mom will stay planted on the couch," Sage replied.

"There're some nice steaks in the fridge on the back porch and there's plenty to go around. Cook them all or they'll go to waste. Potatoes are under the sink if you need them. I should be back in a couple of hours," Gerald said.

"Be careful. The temperature is dropping, and the roads will be solid ice by the time you head back," Sarah said.

"I'll be careful," he promised with a smile and a twinkle in his eye.

Watching what had just unfolded in front of her, Sage wondered if Carol was right and there was something happening between her mom and Gerald.

No, can't be. Ella hasn't even been gone a year. It's too fast for something to happen.

"Sage! Earth to Sage!"

"I'm sorry, Mom. Lost in my thoughts again," Sage said. "Do you need something?"

"No, I was just wondering how things went around here today," she replied.

"It was quiet. I read all day."

"Good. I was afraid our nightly visitor would show up again," Sarah said, yawning.

"I'm going out to get the steaks from the fridge on the porch."

Sarah drifted off while Sage started supper preparations. She set a big kettle on the stove to boil potatoes for mashed potatoes and made a large bowl of green salad with lettuce, tomato wedges, cucumbers, shredded carrots, and onions. Sage kept checking out the kitchen window, anticipating the return of the rest of the gang. When it got dark and three hours had passed, she became concerned and went to wake up her mom.

"Something's wrong," Sage said. "They should have been back by now."

"This is the kind of time you wish you had cell phone service," Sarah replied.

A short time later, two vehicles pulled into the driveway, followed by a cruiser. Sage grabbed her coat and ran outside. As they piled out of the vehicles, Sage noticed Andy was not among them.

THREE

"Where's Andy?" she whispered to Cliff.

"We don't know. He was walking around the parking lot with Rory and myself and the next moment, he was gone. Just vanished into thin air," he replied.

"How could that happen? Did you check all the cars parked there to see if he was inside any of them?" Sage asked.

"We did. We never left the area making sure no one entered or left the parking lot until the police got there. They followed us to the cabin to talk to your mom about her accident today and to ask you about the woman who warned you in the coffee shop."

The others, with the exception of the sheriff, joined Cliff and stood at the back of the SUV. Acting in an official capacity, the sheriff introduced Sage to the officers and took a step back. They spoke with her, took the mystery woman's description, and asked to talk to Sarah.

They disappeared inside and came out a short time later, closing their notebooks.

"We got a picture of your officer from his fiancé. We'll put out a BOLO. Thanks for your help and we'll be in touch if we learn anything," the officer told the sheriff. "How long will you be here?"

"We'll be leaving early Tuesday morning."

"Hopefully we'll have some news by then," the officer said, getting into his cruiser.

They watched them drive away and huddled together to discuss what had happened.

"Can we discuss this inside? I don't want to leave my mom alone for any longer than I have to," Sage asked. "And I have supper already started. I left the steaks for you guys to cook on the grill."

"We can do that," Cliff replied..

The group moved inside and gathered in the kitchen while Sage and Gabby put the finishing touches on supper. Gerald and Cliff had steak duty and went outside to heat up the grill. Gabby seasoned the meat and brought it out.

Shelly sat in front of the fireplace staring into the flames. Her eyes were swollen from crying and she wasn't talking to anyone. Sarah hobbled over and sat down on the hearth next to her. She quietly spoke to the young woman who turned and gave Sarah a hug.

"Steaks are done. Some are cooked to medium, and some are medium rare. If anyone wants it well done let me know and I'll throw one back on the grill until it looks like a charcoal briquet," Gerald said, trying to get a smile out of everyone.

"Come on, you need to eat something," Sarah said, taking Shelly's hand.

Everyone filled their plates and sat around the fireplace. Gerald had fixed a plate for Sarah and delivered it to her after making her sit back down. He stopped at the door and told Barry the food was ready and to come out and make up a plate.

"I'll be right out," he replied.

Gerald went into the kitchen and returned with a plate of food and two beers. He sat on the couch next to Sarah and set his food down on the floor.

"I want to apologize. I very rarely stockpile my beers, but Andy is missing, and it bothers me immensely that we don't have a clue as to why," he said, pointing to the two beers at his feet. "I need to relax so I can clear my mind."

"You have nothing to apologize for," Sarah said. "You're just worried about someone you care about."

"You can't help what happened to Andy," Shelly said quietly.

"I'm going to eat in the bunkroom if that's okay," Barry said.

"Sure, not a problem," Gerald replied.

"I wonder why he doesn't want to eat with us," Gabby said, watching him close the door behind him.

"I think he looks forward to coming here to the cabin to get away from the everyday hassles at home. It's not really upbeat here right now with everything that is going on," Gerald said. "He might want to be where it's quiet."

"That is so sad. He should be having the best years of his life while he's in school," Sarah said.

"He should be," Gerald said, watching the door to make sure Barry didn't come out.

The group sat there in silence. Mouths hung open but no food was being eaten. It was hard for them to fathom a parent acting that way as they all had wonderful, caring parents who supported and loved them.

"We have another storm rolling in tonight," Gerald said, breaking the silence. "They are only predicting three to six inches but we still need to restock the wood bins. Also, if anyone wants to join me, I'll be heading out early in the morning up to the ski lodge to look for Andy."

Everyone agreed to go, and this time Sarah would stay at the cabin to stay off her feet. She said she would be fine and the issue with her ankle wouldn't keep her from handling any situation which arose. Sage didn't really want to leave her mother alone, but Sarah insisted she go with the others to search for their missing friend.

They ate pretty much in silence. There was no joking around or laughing like the night before as everyone was worried about Andy. Sage and Gabby cleaned up the kitchen while the guys finished their beers.

"Not the weekend everyone was planning on having," Cliff said, entering the kitchen with a couple of empty beer bottles.

"No, it's not," Sage agreed. "But let's try and make the best of what's left of it. Hopefully we can find Andy tomorrow and things can return to normal."

"Time to get some shut eye," Cliff replied.

"Kitchen's clean. Cliff, would you help my mom get to her bunk? Unless she wants to sleep on the couch, of course."

"Will do."

Everyone headed for their bunks, including Sarah, so they could get an early start in the morning. While they slept, fresh snow fell. The wind wasn't as wild or as noisy as the previous night, but again, Sage couldn't sleep. Her mind was on the Andy and what could have happened to him. She heard a noise in the kitchen and got up to investigate what was causing it.

Shelly was standing at the counter, mindlessly dipping a teabag in and out of a mug of hot water. She was quietly sobbing.

"Shelly, are you okay?" Sage asked, startling the woman.

"Not really," she whispered.

"I came out to get a cup of tea. May I join you?"

"I guess so."

Sage grabbed a teabag, set it in her mug and went to the kettle on top of the wood stove to get her hot water. She returned to the kitchen to add sugar and a dash of milk to her tea.

"I'm going to stoke the fire and sit there for a bit. Do you want to join me?" Sage asked.

"Okay."

"Great, I'll get the fire going again" Sage said, walking out of the kitchen.

Sage stoked the embers, added a crumpled-up newspaper and when the blaze was going added some wood to build up the fire. She grabbed a blanket off the back of one of the chairs and sat on the couch facing the fireplace. A few minutes later, Shelly came into the living room and sat in the chair opposite the couch where Sage was sitting. Ten minutes passed without either woman uttering a word.

"Why Andy?" Shelly asked.

Sage didn't answer her.

"This was our first vacation together."

"I'm sure it will be the first of many," Sage replied.

"He just gave me my ring last week," she said, holding up her hand to look at her diamond. "He was so funny. He couldn't wait for Valentine's Day to give it to me so he popped the question while we were shoveling his mom's driveway."

"Andy's a great guy. We'll find him, don't you worry," Sage said.

"I'm trying not to, but I can't help it."

"Can you think of any reason, any reason at all, of why anyone would want to hurt him?" Sage asked.

"Everyone loves Andy. I can't think of anyone," Shelly answered.

"The only reason I can come up with for his disappearance is maybe Andy saw the guy who tried to run my mom off the slopes," Sage said. "Go try to get some sleep. You'll need it for tomorrow."

"I'll try, but it won't be easy," Shelly said, standing up. "I have to think positive. The sheriff is a smart man and I know he won't give up until he finds Andy."

"None of us will," Sage assured her.

"Good night," Shelly said, disappearing into the other room, leaving Sage alone in front of the fire.

I hope she gets some sleep because I'm wide awake now.

Sage sipped her tea staring into the fire. The dancing flames gave her something to focus on to clear her mind. She was startled when she turned and saw Barry standing there.

"What's up?" she asked him.

"Just things," he replied. "Can I ask you something?"

"Sure. What do you want to know?"

"Your mom and Gerald. What's up with them?" Barry asked.

"They're friends. They have been since kindergarten."

"Then why is she over at his house all the time?"

"My mom went through a bad divorce many years ago and the people in the town took my dad's side over hers and turned their backs on her. She felt alone and depressed. My mom didn't want Gerald to feel alone after his wife passed. And, my mom is very involved in town matters which a lot of times involves the sheriff's office."

"My mom doesn't see it that way," Barry mumbled.

"What do you mean?" Sage asked.

"It doesn't matter, it's not important," he replied.

"Sometimes people can't change. They are what they are," Sage said. "If you don't like the way she is, make sure you're a different type of person and don't follow in her footsteps."

"I'm trying. That's when I go out and shoot hoops. I've gotten pretty good at it and I may try out for basketball my senior year."

"That would be awesome," Sage said, encouraging his good choices.

Sage wanted so badly to tell Barry that Gerald offered up his house for him to live there, but she knew it wasn't her place to do so. That information would have to come from Gerald himself.

"What do you think happened to Andy?" Barry asked. "Don't treat me like a little kid. Tell me the truth, please."

"My own opinion? I think he saw the person who ran my mom off the slopes. I think he was kidnapped because he was a witness," Sage replied.

"Thank you for being honest with me. But if a person was wearing a black ski mask, why would they take someone who couldn't identify them?""

"It's just a theory. I'm done with my tea and I'm going to bed. Are you going with us in the morning to look for Andy?"

"You bet I am," he replied. "I'm going back to bed now, too. See you in a few hours."

The storm had passed during the night and the sun was shining brightly the next morning. The guys went outside to do a quick shoveling to clear the driveway while the women cooked breakfast.

"Will you be okay if I go with the guys?" Sage asked her mom, flipping blueberry pancakes that were cooking on the griddle.

"I'll be fine," she replied.

A quick breakfast of pancakes and sausages was consumed. Thermoses were filled with hot coffee, and everyone piled into Gerald's vehicle for their trip.

"No one goes anywhere by themselves. Spread out and we'll meet in the lodge in an hour," Gerald instructed the group. "I'm going into the security office even though I believe the local police have already viewed the footage of the parking lots. They don't know Andy and I may spot him where they missed him somewhere."

"We'll break up into pairs and cover all the parking lots," Sage said.

They met back at the lodge, and no one had seen anything which led to Andy's whereabouts. The sheriff had viewed all the footage from the previous day and saw nothing either.

"How does someone just disappear?" Rory asked. "And leave no trace of where they went?"

"It's strange," Sage said, sipping her coffee. "I was warned to be careful about my mom, but not Andy. The only thing that makes any sense is he saw who ran my mom off the slopes and is now paying the price for it."

"What do we do now?' Gabby asked Gerald.

"I guess we let the police take it from here. We can go back to the cabin and get our skis and hit the slopes for a few hours. Yes or no?"

"As bad as I feel about Andy missing, I have to agree. There's not much more we can do," Cliff replied. "I'm in for a few hours of skiing."

"You guys can go skiing; I'm going to stay at the cabin with my mom. Something's not right and I can't put my finger on it," Sage said.

"I'll stay with you at the cabin," Shelly said. "I'm not in the mood to go skiing without Andy."

They pulled into the driveway and Sage noticed the cabin door was wide open.

"What the heck?" she asked, jumping out of the car. "Something's wrong."

FOUR

Sage ran into the cabin, yelling for her mom. No one answered, it was empty. Everything in the living room was turned over as if a struggle had ensued. Sarah's crutches were in the middle of the room, and her mug of coffee had been spilled on the floor in front of the couch.

"Gerald, my mom's gone," she yelled, returning to the door. "Her crutches are here and so is her purse. Her cell phone is on the floor."

"Don't touch anything," he said, entering the door. "Cliff, check out the back door and see if there are any footprints."

"There's none," he reported upon his return. "The snow hasn't been disturbed."

"That's means they were probably watching the cabin when we left and barged in through the front door before Sarah had a chance to lock it," Gerald stated.

"That was hours ago. They have a huge head start on us," Sage said.

Any idea of skiing had gone by the wayside. Gerald excused himself and drove until he could get a signal on his cell phone to call the local police and then returned to the cabin. The group stayed in the kitchen so as not to disturb anything in the living room area before the police arrived.

"I'll be devastated if anything happens to your mom," Gerald said, sitting down next to Sage. "I should have gone with my gut and stayed here with her and let you young folks go search up at the ski lodge."

"You had no way of knowing," Sage replied.

"But I should have, after you saw the face at the window the other night. They were probably hiding in the woods and jumped at the chance when we left Sarah here by herself."

"I guess the woman in the coffee shop was trying to warn me and not issue a threat," Sage said, sighing.

"I have to leave. I promised to meet the police out on the main road in twenty minutes."

"Do you want any of us to go with you?" Sage asked.

"No, I'm doing everything by the book and letting the local police handle this. It's not my jurisdiction and I'm just escorting them to the cabin. If we catch who is responsible for this, there will be no mistakes made which can be used by their attorneys to free their client or clients as the case may be. I'll be back shortly."

"First Andy and now my mom. I don't care if it's only eleven o'clock. I need a glass of wine," Sage said. "My nerves are shot."

"There has to be some kind of connection to this area," Cliff stated. "Someone who lives around here and has a place to hide people after they're taken."

"Or they could have just rented somewhere near here when they found out this was where we were going skiing," Rory added.

"True."

Gerald returned with the two local officers and they went to work in the living room. Everyone watched from the kitchen, not saying a word. They finished up, took a picture of Sarah that Sage had in her purse, and left. Gerald followed them out to their cruiser and they talked for several minutes. He was frowning as he returned to the cabin.

"Not good news?" Sage asked.

"They still don't have anything in the search for Andy and now Sarah was taken out in the middle of nowhere with no cameras around to help."

"I still think it has to be someone who lives close to here. They couldn't bring Andy or Sarah into a hotel or motel without being noticed. They have to own a house or, like Rory said, they have a private rental," Cliff said again.

"I know someone who lives near here," Barry mumbled.

"You do, Barry? Who?" Gerald asked.

"I think one of my uncles lives around here, but I'm not sure exactly where."

"What's his name?" Sage asked.

"I'm sorry, I don't know. I've never met any of my relatives because they all can't stand my mom and stayed away. I don't remember any of them ever visiting us at the house."

"You know, Carol once told me she had many siblings, all brothers. If we can find out her maiden name we can see if any of them are living in this area," Gerald stated.

"Barry, do you know what your mom's maiden name was?" Gabby asked.

"I don't. My mom and I aren't that close. I hardly know anything at all about her family," Barry replied.

"In all the years I lived next door to Carol, I never saw a single relative visit her. Then again, I was at work most days," Gerald stated.

"You do realize that Carol has a massive crush on you? She blames my mom for being at your house all the time as the reason you and she are not together already," Sage said.

"It's true," Barry said.

"I made it quite clear to Carol there would never be anything between us," Gerald replied. "And I told her there was nothing between Sarah and I at least ten times."

"I don't think Carol believes you and has put a plan in place to get rid of my mom. Carol doesn't seem to be a stable person."

"All of this is to say if we don't find proof, we can't say she had anything to do with any of it," Cliff said.

"And sadly, I don't know where to begin looking. I wish we had the internet up here," Sage said. "At least I could feel useful checking into Carol's background and her family members. No offense, Barry."

"None taken," he said.

"I'm going to the station here and see if I can find any information on Carol and her brothers. Hopefully, I'll be back with some good news," Gerald said, standing up.

Sage watched Gerald drive away. She felt helpless. Cliff walked up behind her and put his arms around her waist.

"They'll find her," Cliff stated. "Sarah will be okay. She's a strong woman, just like her daughter."

"I never should have left her here by herself."

"You didn't know anything would happen."

Sage didn't reply and continued to stare out the door.

"I know that look. What else is bothering you?" Cliff asked.

"Andy. If he saw who tried to hurt my mom, he doesn't stand much of a chance of coming out of this alive, if he's not dead already," Sage replied. "It makes me even more afraid for my mom."

"We need to keep a positive outlook. Hopefully, Andy is just being kept somewhere out of the way, so he won't mess up whatever plans the abductors have."

"I hope the people who did this at least have them held together somewhere and they can help each other to escape," Sage said. "It's not going to do any good staring out the door. I guess I can make lunch for everyone and start on the homemade meatballs to go with the spaghetti planned for supper."

"What can I do to help?" Cliff asked, spinning her around and giving her a kiss.

"Nothing. Grab a beer and join the others. I'm sure Gabby will help me, seeing as it's her meatball recipe I'm using."

"I'm not going to do nothing. I will grab a beer, but I'm going to walk around outside and see if I can find anything to help. Maybe they left something behind, or I can find a set of tire tracks that don't belong to any of our vehicles."

"I'll finish in the kitchen and let you know when lunch is ready. After we eat, I'll join you in the search."

"I'll take Rory with me, and we'll concentrate on the front area of the cabin seeing as the snow was undisturbed out back," Cliff, said, grabbing two beers out of the fridge.

Gabby joined Sage in the kitchen. They set out deli meats and cheese with a variety of breads and rolls for lunch. Pickles, individual sized bags of chips and condiments were set on the kitchen island. Sage happened to glance out the kitchen window when she was retrieving the paper plates out of the cabinet.

Gerald had returned from the police station and was talking to Cliff and Rory. The sheriff did not look happy, and Sage had to know why. She grabbed her coat and joined them in the driveway.

"What's wrong?" she asked, joining the group. "Couldn't they find anything on Carol's family?"

"It seems she doesn't have any family members in this area to account for," Cliff replied, relaying what had already been discussed.

"But Barry said he had an uncle in this area," Sage said.

"He might have lived here when Barry was younger and moved away already," Cliff said. "There are no Walkers listed in the Perry area."

"The police are still working on it. They have accounted for all of the siblings except for one, a brother named Brian. All the others live in other states and have alibis for yesterday when Andy went missing and were nowhere in this area today when Sarah was taken."

"You said her maiden name was Walker?" Sage asked.

"Yes, but the family didn't live in Cupston. Carol and her husband moved here after they married," Gerald replied. "In one of our other trips to the cabin, Barry told me his mom said his dad signed the house over to her in exchange for her signing the divorce papers and not contesting it in any way. He wanted a clean break and to have nothing to do with her ever again."

"What will happen to Barry if, I mean when, we find Andy and Sarah and Carol is somehow involved in this mess?" Cliff asked.

"Somehow involved? Seriously?" Sage said.

"I'll do my best to make sure he comes to live with me. He can continue in the same school, keep his friends and try to have as normal a life as possible," Gerald answered. "And I have to agree with Sage. Carol is definitely involved somehow."

"Do you remember the day you came back to the cabin with the police? Did you or the other officers ever mention the person who ran my mom off the slope was dressed in black and had on a black ski mask when he did it?" Sage asked.

"No. it was never addressed. They were more interested in gathering information about Andy. Why?" Gerald asked.

"Last night, Barry came out while I was sitting in front of the fire. He asked me to be truthful with him about what I thought happened to Andy. I told him my theory on why I thought Andy was taken and he responded by asking why they would take someone if they didn't know who the person was that was wearing a black ski mask. I just found it odd," Sage said.

"I don't think it was ever mentioned again after we discussed it standing in the driveway," Gerald replied. "But then again, he was at the ski lodge when Sarah got run off the slopes and we were talking about the person who did it being all dressed in black."

"True, I didn't think of that," Sage muttered. "The only thing I have left to go on is that woman at the coffee shop and why she issued that warning to me.

Who is she and how is she connected to the abductions?"

"Are you going to tell her the other bad news?" Cliff asked Gerald.

"Tell me what?" Sage asked.

"It seems Carol has disappeared. I had my guys go over there to ask her some questions and the place is locked up tight."

"That's a little suspicious, don't you think?" Sage asked.

"Yes. There's only two houses on the street, hers and mine, so there was no one to see when she left," Gerald replied.

"If it is true that Carol is behind this, doesn't it make sense she would be somewhere here in the area to see what was happening?" Rory asked. "It seems likely, to me anyway, that she would have gone to an isolated hotel or motel to stay. I think we should check out the smaller, less popular places around the area and see if she has checked in somewhere under another name."

"Problem is we don't have a picture of her," Gerald stated.

"Oh, but we do. Be right back," Sage said, running for the cabin and returning with her cell phone. "I took this one day when I was over at your house delivering some papers for my mom. I took a picture of the lilacs in your yard and Carol was standing right there at the back of your car waiting for me to leave."

"This is perfect. We can each take a picture of your phone and we'll have something to show the desk clerks," Gerald stated. "Let's eat lunch and head out. I think I need to be in one car and at least one of the guys in the other car in case trouble arises."

Over lunch it was decided that Sage, Cliff, and Barry would go in Cliff's car and the others would go in Gerald's SUV. Not having any cell reception, they returned to the old ways and took a phone book that was in the cabin for renters and made two lists of all the hotels, motels, and ski lodges within an hour radius of the cabin.

"You know there are hundreds of hunting cabins in the area. If Carol does know someone locally they could be staying at one of those instead of some-where public," Gerald stated.

"That does make more sense. But how would they be able to explain Andy and Sarah?" Rory said. "At least we can rule out all the places on our lists as a starting point."

"I know the cell reception is sketchy but try to check in as often as you can," Gerald said, climbing into the car. "Cliff, did you lock up the cabin?"

"I did."

"Great! Let's go find our missing friends," he replied.

Each car headed up the mountain until the road split and they each went the way of their listings. Once they were up in the area of the lodgings, the cell phone reception was fine and they were able to check in once they had crossed three places off their lists. An hour passed and there was no sign of Carol anywhere.

Cliff pulled up in front of The Lonely Cub Ski Lodge. It was a smaller lodge and nowhere near any of the ski slopes. They advertised privacy and catered to honeymooners and private parties, but this time of year they filled their rooms with people in the area enjoying the skiing.

Sage hopped out of the car, phone in hand, and opened the lodge door. She stopped short in her tracks as she was face to face with the woman from the coffee shop who was on her way out, suitcase in hand.

"Oh, you're not going anywhere," Sage ordered.

"Get out of my way!" she demanded.

"Cliff, she's the one! She was at the coffee shop and warned me about harm coming to my mom," Sage yelled, grabbing the woman's arm.

FIVE

"You're not going anywhere," Cliff said, taking hold of the woman's other arm as she struggled to get away. "Where are Sarah and Andy?"

"I don't know what you're talking about," she replied, still attempting to break free. "Where is my mom? You told me to watch over her and now she is missing."

"Let's take her inside. I need to call the sheriff and the local authorities," Cliff said, dragging the fighting woman back inside the lodge as the other guests watched wide-eyed.

Cliff grabbed the woman's suitcase and he sat her in the corner of the lobby, standing guard over her while Sage went to talk to the desk clerk and request she place a call to a Sheriff Benton. As much as Sage wanted to question the woman, she knew it had to be done the right way to make any kidnapping case stick. She dialed Gerald's number next and told him where they were and that they found the woman from the coffee shop. He promised to get there as quickly as possible.

"Sheriff Benton will be here in about twenty minutes," Sage said, returning to the group.

The woman started quietly sobbing which turned into a full blown stream of tears.

"I don't know what he would have done if he found out I tried to warn you. You have no idea what kind of people you are dealing with"

"Who?" Sage asked. "What is your name?"

She looked at each one in the group and then sat there, head down not saying another word. They waited in silence until Benton arrived with another deputy.

"Sheriff White informed me this morning you would be out looking for Carol today. Is she here?" he asked Sage.

"We don't know. We haven't had a chance to show the desk clerk her picture and we haven't questioned this woman, as we were waiting for you to get here. It is your jurisdiction."

"Can I borrow your phone?" Benton asked Sage. "I want to go show the clerk Carol's picture."

Benton rejoined the group.

"The desk clerk doesn't remember seeing Carol, but she just came on at seven this morning and wasn't here last night when the registration was signed. The woman sitting over there registered under the name of Marsha Walker."

"Walker? Isn't that Carol's maiden name?" Cliff asked.

"It is, and now we have a connection to Carol's family. Right before I left for here we found out that Carol's brother, Brian Walker, lives in Forest Hills, twenty miles from here," Benton stated. "Marsha is Brian Walker's wife."

"So can we assume that Brian Walker was the man dressed in black who tried to hurt my mom?" Sage asked. "And this woman knew what was going to happen and she tried to warn me? But why would she go against her husband?"

"That's what we need to find out," Benton replied.

"Let me try to question her," Sage said. "It might not be as scary for her to talk to another woman."

"Go ahead. She might respond to you better than any of us, otherwise she wouldn't have tried to warn you," Benton said.

Sage sat down next to Marsha who didn't even look up to acknowledge her presence.

"Marsha, why did you try to warn me about harm that might come to my mom?"

Silence.

"It was your husband who tried to run my mom off the slopes when she was skiing, wasn't it?"

Marsha looked up at Sage.

"Why are you here at the lodge and not at home?" Sage asked, taking the woman's hand.

"I was hiding here."

"Hiding from who? Your husband?"

"Yes, him and Carol."

"Is my mom still alive?" Sage asked, choking on the words as she said them.

"Yes."

"Did your husband take Andy because he caught up with him at the ski lodge after the incident?"

"Yes, but that's not the only reason," Marsha whispered, tearing up.

"What do you mean?" Sage asked.

"I can't say any more," Marsha whispered.

A deputy entered the lodge and waved Benton over to talk to him. Marsha watched them intently but still didn't say anything.

"My deputy has discovered that your husband owns a small parcel of land under another name on the outskirts of Forest Hills. As we speak, I have a team of men going to check the area as we found out there is a small structure on the property. If we find the two missing people there, and find out you knew they were there, you will be charged along with Carol and Brian," Benton said to Marsha.

Marsha's eyes grew wide.

"They are there. He left them there," Marsha whispered, reaching for a trash barrel next to the table. "I feel sick."

"Brian left them there to die?"

"He did, but Carol was in on it, too," Marsha whispered.

"In on what?" Benton asked.

"Can you guarantee me protection?" Marsha asked. "I was on my way to running far away when I ran into Sage at the door. I don't want to be anywhere near those people ever again."

"If you cooperate, we will put you in protective custody," Benton stated.

"My husband owns an insurance agency. For years he has been filing false claims and collecting money left and right," Marsha said. "And then, he and Carol cooked up a scheme a while ago to take out fake life insurance policies on your mom with double indemnity if she died by accident. That's why they tried to make her death look like a skiing accident. They forged her signature on the two policies, for a million each."

"It had to be right around the time Ella died and Sarah started coming to my house more frequently," Gerald stated. "And so did Carol."

"Carol said it was a bonus if Sarah died. Carol blamed her that Gerald and she weren't a couple, but spending the money they collected from her death, laying on a warm tropical beach, would heal her pain."

"Andy? What about Andy?" Gerald asked.

"He had nothing to do with anything. He was at the wrong place at the wrong time. When Brian returned to his car, he took off his ski mask and black coat and threw them in the trunk of his car. He turned to see Andy standing there watching him. They got in a struggle and Brian hit him with a ski pole on the side of the head, knocking him out. Brian stuffed him in the trunk and drove off before your other friends blocked the exit."

"How would they collect the insurance money? It would be traced back to your husband's company," Sage asked.

"My husband has many friends, lowlifes that help him collect the fraudulent claims all over the country. They use many aliases and have the system down pretty good. They get a cut, and everyone walks away happy. This was going to be their big score. Carol and Brian were going to take the money and disappear to somewhere with no extradition policies with the United States."

"Carol was just going to leave Barry behind?" Gerald asked. looking at the boy's crestfallen face.

"She knew you would take him in because you told her you would."

"I did say that to her," Gerald admitted, looking at Barry. "And I meant it. I want you to stay with me, if you chose to, while you're still in school."

"I told them I wanted no part of their schemes and decided to run away."

Marsha looked from one face to another.

"Can someone take Barry for a short walk?" Marsha asked.

"You don't have to hide anything from me, Aunt Marsha. I can call you that, right?" Barry asked. "I never had an aunt or uncle before."

"Yes, you can, but I'm not sure you need to hear this," she replied.

"I need to hear the truth," he said. "I'm old enough."

"I guess you will find out sooner or later. There is a reason your dad never came back for you. The night he went to the house to collect the signed divorce papers, he never left again."

"My dad didn't desert me?"

"No, he didn't. He loved you more than life itself. The house was in his name and he was going to sell it to give you both a fresh start somewhere else. He told your mother she had a month to get out of the house and she decided to take a different direction. She killed him, never filed the divorce papers, and stayed in the house telling everyone that he deserted you to cover her tracks."

"My dad didn't desert me. Do you how happy that makes me feel?" Barry said, smiling. "And he loved me."

Gerald put his arm around Barry's shoulders and gave him a smile.

"I was waiting until I could get far away from Carol and Brian before I told you the rest of the story. Your dad knew I couldn't stand Carol, and would watch out for you, so he confided many things in me before he was killed. His will, which was written before he decided to sell the house, is hidden in a secret spot in the house and in it he left everything to you. I guess as the house was never sold, it belongs to you. Your mother did her darndest to try to find it to contest it, but she never could."

"Why didn't you tell someone this before now?" Benton asked.

"It took me thirty-four years to work up the courage to leave. I think at this point, my husband doesn't care that I'm gone because he can start his new life being single without anyone tying him down."

"So, my mom was singled out because of petty jealousy?" Sage asked.

"Unfortunately, yes. It started out that way but later became all about the money they could collect. I really think Gerald would have ended up in the back yard, too, if they got married. When Carol got tired of him and had enough insurance policies on him to make it worth her while, she would have killed him."

"I wasn't sure what they were going to do to her so I tried to warn you. I was hoping you wouldn't go to the cabin if you thought your mom was in danger. I couldn't stick around to tell you any details, as my husband was waiting in the car for me."

"If you knew where they were being held, why didn't you tell someone?" Benton asked.

"I was going to as soon as I got away this morning. I knew when I didn't go home last night, Brain and Carol would be looking for me."

"And now they have probably moved my mom and Andy," Sage said, biting her lower lip.

"I just got word," one of the deputies said, approaching the group. "They found the woman, Sarah Fletcher, in the shack. The deputy is not there."

"Is my mom okay?"

"She's cold but fine, and on her way to the Perry Hospital. She said they drugged both her and Andy and dropped them in the shack yesterday morning. They were tied and chained to pipes. They stayed snuggled together for warmth but later in the afternoon, they came back and took Andy away."

"Did she say who they were?" Gerald asked.

"She was able to tell us it was Carol Steiner but she didn't know who the male was," the deputy answered.

"Where would they take him, Marsha? You must have some idea," Sage asked the woman.

"After the skiing attempt failed, the plan was to make it look like they got lost and froze to death in the woods. There is a cave on the property that Brian doesn't know I know about. I would bet my own life he put your friend there," Marsha replied.

"Are the men still at the shack?" Benton asked.

"They are."

"Tell them to stay put and we will be there in twenty minutes. Marsha is going to show us where the cave is," Benton stated. "Aren't you?

"I will, but you have to hide me until you arrest my husband," Marsha pleaded.

"Let's go. Gerald, I'll let you know if we find your man," Benton said.

"I'll be at the hospital checking on Sarah. Come on, Sage, let's go see your mom."

On the ride to the hospital, Sage messaged the other car and told them they could call off their search. Gabby didn't answer right away, and Sage thought it was odd but then chalked it up to the fact that cell service up here was sketchy at best.

They arrived at the hospital and were shown to Sarah's room. Benton had called ahead of their arrival and told the hospital they were coming, and that it was okay to let them see the patient. They entered the cubicle and upon seeing her mom, Sage started to cry. The crying woke Sarah up and Sage rushed forward to hug her.

"Don't cry, I'm fine," Sarah said, brushing away her daughter's tears. "Gerald, Cliff, some skiing vacation, huh?"

"We're just glad you're okay," Gerald said, walking to the bed and taking hold of her hand. "It's only the middle of February and we can come back up again once your ankle is better. Or next year and the year after that."

"Andy? Have they found him yet?"

"Not yet but they have a good lead as to where he is being hidden," Gerald replied.

Barry walked up to the side of the bed.

"I'm so sorry my mom did this to you," he said, quietly.

"Don't you worry about it. You had nothing to do with it and everyone knows that," she replied, patting the back of his hand. "Everything's going to turn out okay."

"I heard Carol and that guy talking. They were going to stage my death to collect insurance money on fake policies. I was horrified. I tried to fight them when they came to take Andy away, but I got hit on the back of the head and blacked out. When I woke up he was gone," Sarah stated.

"This was never about you personally, only about the money they were going to collect," Gerald said. "You were their big score as they say."

"Carol said I was a bonus kill. Can you imagine that? A bonus kill? What kind of person have you been living next to all this time?"

"Scary, isn't it. I guess you never know who your neighbors really are," Gerald said. "Especially when they have a body buried in the back yard."

"What? Who's buried in the back yard?" Sarah asked.

"We'll tell you everything when we spring you from here," Sage said.

"I have to step outside. Rory's calling me," Cliff said.

Gerald pulled up a chair and sat next to the bed, not letting go of Sarah's hand. Their smiles told Sage everything she needed to know. There was a spark growing between her mom and Gerald. Carol had been right the whole time.

"Excuse me. I'm going to see if Cliff is still talking to Rory and where they are," Sage said. "Are you going to stay here, Barry?"

"Yeah, if that's okay," he replied, plopping into a chair in the corner of the room.

Sage approached Cliff in the lobby just as he was hanging up the call.

"Is everything okay?" she asked.

"It's more than okay. In their travels they passed a car that Carol was a passenger in and they followed it, being careful to stay out of sight so they wouldn't spook them. They followed them to these little rental cabins that weren't even listed in the phone book. They watched them check in and go to one of the back cabins far from the main road. Rory called it in and half the Perry force showed up to take them into custody."

"I think it's safe to say that when Marsha disappeared they knew they weren't going to get any insurance money and decided to go on the run instead," Sage replied.

"Oh, they got their hands on some money. When they were arrested, the officers found a suitcase full of money. Brian had cleaned out the safe of the insurance company he owns. They had plenty of money to leave the country and never be seen again," Cliff said.

"They found Andy," Gerald announced, entering the lobby. "They're bringing him in by ambulance as we speak."

"Is he okay?" Cliff asked.

"He has some frostbite and his body temp is lower than it should be, but the paramedics think he will make a full recovery. He remembered his survival training from Scouts and covered himself in leaves and moss trying to retain his body heat. The paramedics said if he hadn't done what he did he would probably be dead."

"What's going to happen to Marsha?" Sage asked.

"I don't know. She helped lead them to Andy so that's in her favor."

"And she did try to warn me about the danger to my mom," Sage added.

"I believe if she agrees to testify against the other two, she will walk away with a slap on the wrist," Gerald stated. "I already talked to an attorney back home and I'm going to become Barry's legal guardian so he will be living with me for now. If he agrees to it. Or, if Marsha gets immunity for testifying, she could move in with Barry as his legal family.

She has nowhere to go right now so it might work out for the both of them."

"That means, with murder charges added on to all the other charges Carol faces, she'll be going away for a long time," Cliff stated.

"As is her brother for all his insurance fraud. Marsha won't have anything to fear once those two go through the court system and are sentenced," Gerald replied.

"That's awesome news," Sage said. "I'm sure Barry will jump at the chance to stay with you. Although, he did look pretty happy when he called Marsha aunt."

"I think it will be a great deal for Barry no matter who he chooses."

"The others are on their way here," Cliff said, reading a new message on his phone. "They're about five minutes away."

"I'm going in and sit with Sarah. They are keeping her overnight just as a precaution because of the whack she received on her head. And I want to be out back when Andy's ambulance pulls in. Let me know when the others get here so I can come out and get Shelly."

"We'll be right here waiting for them," Sage said.

"Aren't you going in and sit with your mom?" Cliff asked, watching Gerald walk away.

"No. I think love has worked its magic on my mom and Gerald and anyone else in the room would be invisible to them," Sage said, smiling.

"You mean…"

"Yes, I think Carol was right."

"Well, tomorrow is Valentine's Day and love is in air," Cliff said, giving her a hug.

"It is, isn't it? I forgot all about it being Valentine's Day."

"I didn't," Cliff said, pulling a ring box out of his pocket. "I planned on doing this tomorrow night in front of the fire but right now, at this time, it's a little more private."

"Oh, Cliff."

"I know I gave you a promise ring but it's not the same as an engagement ring."

"It was to me," she whispered.

"Sage Fletcher," he said, getting down on one knee and flipping open the ring box to show her a gorgeous two carat heart shaped diamond with three red rubies on either side of it. "Will you marry me?"

"Of course I will," she answered, smiling as he put the ring on her finger.

He stood up and they kissed, oblivious to anyone else around them. Gabby led the way through the emergency room doors. The rest of the group followed behind her into the hospital, witnessing their friend's kiss.

"Hey, get a room," Rory said, joking with his friend.

"We're engaged!" Sage squealed, holding up her hand with the ring on it.

"Now we have two weddings to plan," Gabby said, giving her best friend a huge hug.

"Maybe three," Sage said, laughing at the look her friend was giving her. "I'll explain later."

Printed in Great Britain
by Amazon

42247632R00057